WHY IS SNOW SO WHITE?

Written by Margarita Moksin

Illustrated by Piotrek Antoniak

Why Is Snow So White?

Written by Margarita Moksin
Illustrated by Piotrek Antoniak

Published by Cincinnati Book Publishing
Cincinnati, Ohio

Anthony W. Brunsman, President and CEO
Sue Ann Painter, Vice president and Executive editor
Cover and book design: Greg Eckel

www.cincybooks.com

ISBN 978-0-9995747-2-0

Printed in the United States of America
First Edition, 2017

To purchase additional copies online,
visit www.lovesomi.com

Manufactured by Thomson-Shore, Dexter, MI (USA); RMA25NS012, January, 2018

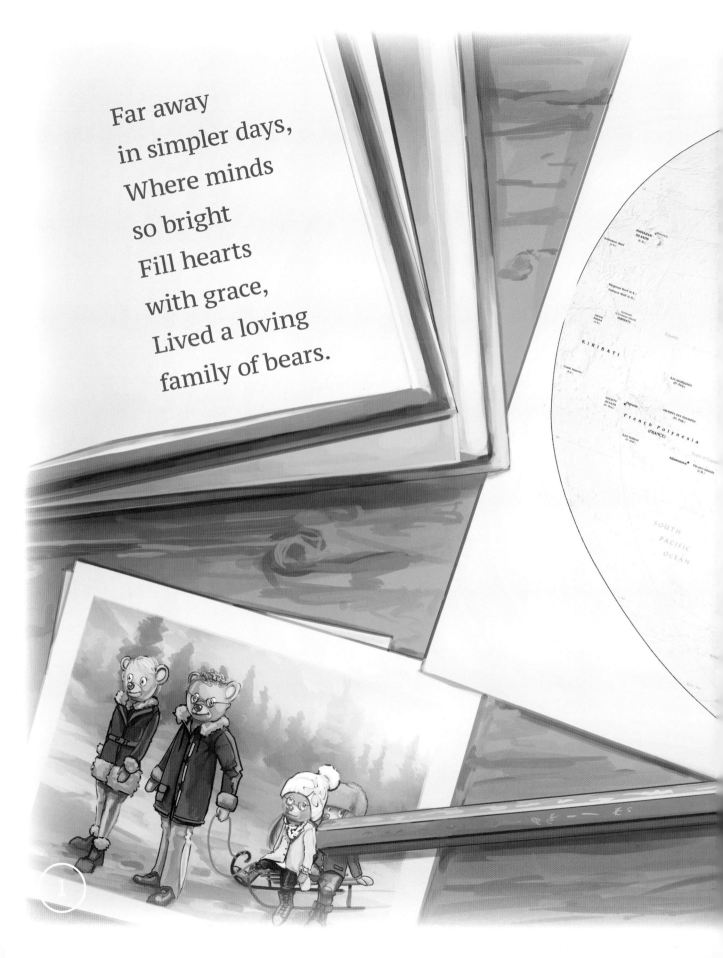

Far away
in simpler days,
Where minds
so bright
Fill hearts
with grace,
Lived a loving
family of bears.

Mom and Dad, two smiling faces,
Enjoy fun learning day and night.

Travel to many different places,
Explore, discover with delight.

One morning, whispering and glaring,
White winter came to forest's sight.

Warm trees revealed
the coats they're wearing.
Snow sparkled with
its purest light.

Mom and Dad inspired greatly
entered Mishka's room to say:

"Have you seen such beauty lately?
Please, let's go outside to play."

6

"Fun to roll down the hill and to jump in the snow.
Riding fast in the sled, fun to glide till you fly."

"Mommy, please may I stay.
Do you think I should go?
Home is cozy and warm.
No, no, no Daddy why?"

8

"When I was a little boy I enjoyed laughing and skiing outside with my friends."

"We'll go all together,
Sofulya will join.
Who knows how
our discovery ends."

"This sweater is itchy,
the boots are too big."

"This hat keeps on falling,
I cannot see a thing."

"Are we ready–let's go!
I'm first on the sled.
Mishka, please pull first
Then I'll pull instead."

Wet snow is so deep,
Makes it too hard to walk.
"I'm cold. Hill is steep.
When I fall...ground is soft!"

Looking silly on the ground,
Fixing hat from falling,
"Mommy, why is snow so white?"
Mishka whispered sprawling.

"Wonderful question,
my darling, you see
Patience always finds ways
to new curiosity."

Clear snowflake is
a tiny piece of ice.
Allows light to travel
through and out.

Each snowflake falls down
without thinking twice,
Always lays randomly
on the ground.

Snow's soft fluffy bulk
cannot pass the light
Bright crystal instead
reflects, intertwines.

We see a pure painting
of lovely white
When every existing
color combines.

As snowflakes landed on her nose,
Sofulya exclaimed in warm delight:

"Mishka, look how interesting up close
Did you ever see two snowflakes alike?"

20

They begin as a cloud high above in the sky
Cold weather then freezes drops to ice.
Humidity, temperature change as they fly,
Little crystals attach, shaping them really nice.

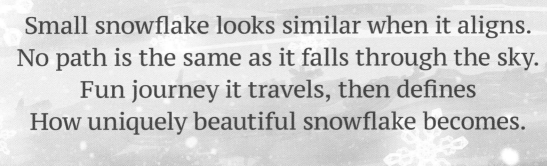

Small snowflake looks similar when it aligns.
No path is the same as it falls through the sky.
Fun journey it travels, then defines
How uniquely beautiful snowflake becomes.

Just as a snowflake's, your path is distinct.
Discover and try exciting new things.

Be patient, determined, kind, and unique,
Experience everything the world has to bring.

Bear family adored outside
As stars were shining really bright...

Kind memories
keep you warm inside.
Mommy and Daddy were,
as always, right.

In loving memory of Ilya.

THE END